WISHES DON'T COME TRUE

by
Brenda Bellingham

Illustrated by
Carol Wakefield

MONDO

For information contact:
MONDO Publishing
980 Avenue of the Americas
New York, New York 10018
Visit our web site at http://www.mondopub.com

Printed in the United States of America
First Mondo printing, January 2000
06 07 08 09   9 8 7 6 5 4 3

ISBN 1-57255-791-5

Designed by Mina Greenstein

Contents

Chapter 1

Jeff's Wish

"Look!" Jeff cried. "It's a four-leaf clover."

"Make a wish, Jeff," said Tilly Perkins.

They were at the edge of the playground looking for a lost baseball. Tilly knelt on the grass next to Jeff.

Some of the other fourth graders came to see what was keeping Jeff and Tilly.

"What do you wish for most in the whole world?" Tilly asked.

"A kitten," answered Jeff. He didn't even have to think about it.

"Your wish is granted," said Tilly Perkins.

"I'll give you a cat. We have some on our farm."

"Lots of people have cats to give away," said Poppy Rose. "You don't have to waste your wish."

"You can say that again," said Sally. "Our street is full of cats."

"The cat woman has a zillion of them," said Bruno.

"She does not," cried Jeff. "She has five."

"Wish for a dirt bike, Jeff," said Bruno.

"It's too late," said Tilly Perkins. "He already wished."

"Wishes never come true, anyway," said Sally.

The bell rang and they had to go into school.

"Who would like to read from his or her journal?" asked Mrs. Frank, the fourth grade teacher.

Tilly Perkins's hand shot up. She got up and stood at the front of the room. As usual, her tights twisted around her skinny legs like corkscrews. Today they had green knees, too. "You might be wondering why I'm wearing a skirt," read Tilly.

Not really, thought Jeff. *It's more of a surprise when she doesn't wear one. Tilly Perkins does farm chores in a skirt. She runs races in a skirt. She climbs trees in a skirt. No wonder she looks like a flower that's been blown around by the wind.*

"Today is a special day," Tilly went on. "My mom and dad are going on an African safari."

"Is that true?" asked Poppy Rose.

"No way," said Sally. "You can't fool me, Tilly Perkins. I'm going to be a lawyer, like my dad. An African safari costs a bundle. Your parents can't afford it."

"They won a prize," said Tilly Perkins. "They will get to see all kinds of wild animals. It's a wish come true. But the prize is only for two. So I need a place to stay." She looked around.

No one said anything.

Did Tilly Perkins look disappointed?

Did Tilly Perkins look discouraged?

No, she did not. Tilly Perkins never looked downhearted. She gave everyone a bright, friendly smile.

Tilly Perkins would invite any one of us to stay

at the farm, thought Jeff. *We wouldn't have to ask twice.*

"You can come to my house," he said, "if you don't mind sleeping in the attic. My mom and dad made a guest room up there. It has its own bathroom."

Tilly grinned at Jeff. Her eyes twinkled. "I love attics," she said. "It's like being a bird. You can see the whole world from an attic window."

"Don't be crazy, Tilly Perkins," said Bruno. "You have to go up in a spaceship if you want to see the whole world."

"Jeff, you should ask your parents first," said Poppy Rose. "They might not want a kid in the guest room. She might mess it up."

"Tilly Perkins might fall out of the window," said Sally. "Then her parents will sue your parents, Jeff. It could cost a bundle. You'll need a lawyer. Here's my card."

"Bruno, your turn to read," said Mrs. Frank. Bruno groaned.

Jeff didn't listen to Bruno. Maybe he should

have asked his parents before he invited Tilly. He hoped they wouldn't say no. Tilly's feelings would be hurt. Luckily, when he told them, they smiled.

"Mrs. Perkins phoned us this morning," said his mom. "It's all arranged."

"Will Tilly bring her animals?" asked Jeff.

"No way," said his dad. "What do you think this is, Noah's Ark? A neighbor is going to feed the farm animals. He'll look after Tilly's pets, too."

Too bad, thought Jeff. *Now Tilly won't be able to leave one of her cats behind by mistake. I guess Sally is right. Wishes don't come true.*

Chapter 2

The Calico Cat

On the first day of Tilly's visit, the roar of Mr. Fesku's motorcycle woke Jeff. The Feskus lived next door. In the winter, Mr. Fesku drove to work in a car. When spring came, he flung open the doors of his motorcycle shed.

"Like letting the horse out of the barn," Jeff's dad said. "But a horse would be a lot quieter."

Tilly Perkins bounded into Jeff's room and leaned out of his window. Jeff was supposed to put the screen in for the summer, but he'd forgotten. *There's lots of time anyway*, he thought. *It's still spring.*

Jeff pointed at the yard next door. "Look,

there's the calico cat from up the road," he said. "It belongs to the cat woman. It shouldn't be in the Feskus' yard. They don't like cats."

"A house isn't a home without a cat on the mat," said Tilly. "That's what my dad says."

"I wish my dad thought that," said Jeff.

There was a sudden crash. The Feskus' back door flew open. Mrs. Fesku ran out. She tossed a broom at the calico cat. The cat yowled.

"Get out of here, you beast," yelled Mrs. Fesku, "and don't come back."

The cat fled over the fence into Jeff's backyard. Jeff raced down the stairs. Tilly came right behind Jeff. She almost stepped on his heels. The cat jumped onto Jeff's picnic table. It licked its fur in a worried way. Jeff scooped it up. The cat climbed up his shoulder and rubbed its head against his cheek. It said a lot of little meows to tell Jeff how scared it felt.

"Don't worry, cat," said Jeff. "You're safe now."

"What a pretty cat," Tilly said. She took the cat from Jeff and cuddled it. "She's going to have kittens."

"How do *you* know?" asked Jeff. "You don't even know if it's a girl."

"A female," said Tilly.

Sometimes, thought Jeff, *Tilly Perkins is a bit of a pain. She thinks she knows everything.* "We'd better take her home," he said. He took the cat from Tilly.

"She likes you," Tilly said. "She's purring." Tilly wasn't really a pain. Jeff took the cat up to his bedroom while he got dressed. Then they took the cat home.

"The cat woman lives on the other side of the Feskus," he said. "Right at the end of the street, next to the hill."

There were no houses across the street from Jeff's—only a steep hill with trees, and a concrete wall to stop people from falling down the hill. Jeff rang the cat woman's doorbell.

The cat woman answered. She was small and slim— about the same size as Tilly Perkins. Today she wore calf-length pants and a man's cloth cap, the kind of clothes worn by golfers in old movies. *She's probably older than my grandma,* thought Jeff.

The cat woman didn't open the door wide. She peered through a narrow opening. "No thanks," she said. "I don't want any."

"We're not selling anything," said Jeff. "We've brought one of your cats home."

The cat woman reached out and took the calico cat.

"Mrs. Fesku threw a broom at her," Jeff said. "The Feskus don't like cats in their yard."

"Fools!" the cat woman said, and she shut the door.

Jeff felt hurt.

Did Tilly Perkins look upset?

Did Tilly Perkins look unhappy?

No, she did not. Tilly Perkins understood. "She's worried about her cat," she said.

The door whisked open again.

"I mean, the Feskus!" shouted the cat woman. "How do they think I can keep her home? She's going to have kittens. She wants to hunt mice."

"You were right," Jeff said to Tilly. Kittens! A little thrill of excitement ran through his body. Maybe he would get his wish after all.

Chapter 3

The Cat Woman

"Come in and have some milk and cookies," said the cat woman. She opened the door just enough for them to squeeze through. "What are your names?" she asked.

"I'm Jeff Brown," Jeff said. "I live on the other side of the Feskus."

"I'm Tilly Perkins," said Tilly. "I'm visiting Jeff."

"You can call me Gribble," said the cat woman, "not Mrs. or Miss or Ms., just Gribble. This is Gladys." She nodded at the calico cat.

Gribble has a voice like a frog, thought Jeff. *Not the chirrupy kind that sing in spring ponds; the bullfrog kind. And her house smells of cats—a little bit—and something else; kind of fishy.* Jeff wasn't sure he wanted milk and cookies. With a hop, skip, and a jump, Tilly Perkins followed Gribble down the hall. She pulled out a chair next to the kitchen table and plonked down on it. Jeff sat down, too. He didn't want to hurt Gribble's feelings.

Gribble poured two glasses of milk. Then she filled a row of bowls on the floor. "Here, kitty, kitty," she called, "snack time!"

There was a flurry of mewing cats. The furry mass came to rest in front of the bowls—one cat per bowl.

"I told Poppy Rose there were only five cats," Jeff murmured. He looked at Gladys. "But soon there will be more," he said. "Then that won't be true."

Did Tilly Perkins tell Jeff he was wrong?

Did Tilly Perkins tell Jeff to count again?

No, she did not. Tilly Perkins didn't care how many cats Gribble had. "What beautiful cats!"she said. "Their coats shine. What's the name of that one?" She pointed to a large, smug-looking, ginger cat.

"Luther," answered Gribble.

Luther ran up the curtains. He hung there for a moment and looked to see if they were watching. Then he walked on tiptoe across the curtain rail and ran down the other curtain.

"Luther is a very athletic cat," said Gribble.

"Most people would be mad at a cat that climbs curtains," said Jeff.

"It's natural for cats to climb," Tilly said.

A third cat, a kittenish tabby with a small, pointed face, pounced on Gladys.

"That's Bud," said Gribble, "our youngest. He likes to tease. He's very playful."

Two half-grown black cats with white markings chased each other's tails.

"Those are the twins," said Gribble.

Gladys jumped onto Jeff's lap. She purred and purred. Jeff stroked her. "Gladys talks the most," he said. "Which cat is the father of her kittens?"

"None of these," said Gribble. "She was expecting when I found her. Someone had thrown her out."

"Oh, poor thing," said Jeff.

"You can have one of her kittens," said Gribble.

Gladys's kitten! thought Jeff. *The next best thing to Gladys herself.* Then he remembered. It was no use wishing. "I can't have a cat," he said.

Gribble glared at him. "I don't give kittens to just anybody," she said.

Tilly Perkins spoke up. "Jeff wants a kitten more than anything," she said. "But his mom and dad won't let him."

"Rotten parents," said Gribble.

"Oh, no!" said Jeff. "They're really not."

"Mad," said Gribble.

"No," said Jeff. "You don't understand."

"No," said Gribble. "I don't."

"Well," said Jeff, "a lot of people don't like cats."

"I don't believe it!" croaked Gribble.

"I'm afraid it's true," said Tilly. "They want to have cats licensed."

"And make people keep them on leashes, like dogs," said Jeff.

"Sour grapes!" said Gribble.

"It's not only dog owners," said Jeff. "Not especially. All kinds of people phone City Hall.

Some write letters to the mayor. Some even come to see him. And my dad is the assistant to the mayor. So he's the one who has to deal with them. It puts Dad in a bad mood."

Gribble gave a kind of snort.

Tilly looked thoughtful. "Jeff, maybe I can teach your dad to like cats," she said.

"He already likes cats," said Jeff. "What he doesn't like is people giving him a bad time about cats."

"You can't tie up a cat," said Tilly. "They have to be free. It's the way they're made."

"It's hard to make some people understand that," said Jeff.

"Birdbrains," said Gribble.

Gribble's a prickly person, thought Jeff. *But she does like cats.*

"Someone should teach those cat haters a lesson," said Tilly. "It's not fair to Jeff."

Uh, oh! thought Jeff. *What does she have in mind? You never know with Tilly Perkins. Maybe Sally was right. I* do *need a lawyer.*

Chapter 4

Horace

After their ball game on Saturday morning, Bruno, Sally, and Poppy Rose walked home with Jeff and Tilly. Outside Jeff's house, they met Mrs. Fesku. She was pushing her toddler, Horace, in his stroller.

"Jeff, where's your mother?" she asked.

"Shopping," said Jeff.

"Oh, dear," said Mrs. Fesku. "I wondered if she might watch Horace. My mother is ill. I have to go to the hospital, and Horace's dad is at work." She looked worried. "I've tried some of the teenagers, but they all seem to be busy."

Bruno looked at his watch. "Oops," he said,

"I just remembered. My mom wants to take me shopping. I need new sneakers."

"I have to get home, too," said Poppy Rose. "We're going over to my grandma's."

"Well, got to run," said Sally. "Dad wants me to help him paint the fence."

Bruno, Sally, and Poppy Rose melted away like ice in springtime.

No one wants to babysit Horace, thought Jeff. *They call him Horror.*

"Jeff and I will babysit Horace," Tilly said.

Tilly Perkins is a very kind girl, thought Jeff. *But she doesn't know Horace.* He tried to think of an excuse. None came to mind.

Horace had a round face, round curls, and big, round eyes. Horace was a very round child. Tilly Perkins played peek-a-boo with him. Horace giggled. *Maybe he isn't as bad as people say,* thought Jeff.

Mrs. Fesku took them into her house. She gave them a few quick lessons on the care and feeding of Horace. "If you let Horace out of the stroller, use the baby minder," she said. "Then he can't run into the road."

Baby minder! It looked like a dog leash to Jeff.

First, they had to give Horace his lunch. Tilly made sandwiches while Jeff watched Horace. Jeff turned on the TV.

"Wow," he said. "My dad's on TV. A reporter is talking to him about the cat problem. Dad doesn't like reporters. He calls them news hounds. He says they chase him like a pack of dogs."

Tilly came to watch Mr. Brown on TV. She and Jeff forgot all about Horace until they heard a crash. They ran into the kitchen to see what had happened.

Horace was standing on the counter. Chocolate cookies rained on his head. They spilled onto the counter and made cookie puddles on the floor.

"Horace!" cried Tilly. She sprinted to catch him before he fell. Chocolate cookies crunched under her feet.

"Cookie," screamed Horace. "Want cookie."

"Give him a cookie," said Jeff. "It'll keep him quiet while we clean up the mess."

Horace wanted four cookies—two in each hand.

"Okay, Horace," said Jeff. "Go and watch TV while you eat your cookies." He found a cartoon program for Horace to watch.

Jeff and Tilly picked up the cookies. Jeff dusted off the whole ones that fell on the counter and put them back in the package.

Tilly swept up the crushed cookies. She put the crumbs and broken cookies in a bag. "This way they won't go to waste," she said. "Gribble's cats will enjoy them."

"Let's watch TV with Horace while we eat," said Jeff. "Maybe Dad's still on."

But Horace wasn't watching TV. He was feeding the fish in his dad's fish tank—with bits of chocolate cookie.

"No, Horace!" cried Jeff. "Fish don't eat cookies. Now the tank is full of cookie crumbs. Your dad will have to clean it out. Bad boy."

Horace began to holler. His mouth made a huge, round "O."

"Horace isn't a bad boy," said Tilly. "He was sharing his cookies with the fish. He's sweet."

She gave him a big, noisy kiss on his fat cheek.

Only Tilly Perkins would think Horace is sweet, thought Jeff. He lifted Horace down from the bookcase. "Horace is going to be a mountain climber when he grows up," he said. "Let's take him for a walk. That'll keep him out of trouble."

They put one end of Horace's leash around his wrist. Tilly wore the other end. In the street they met Bud.

"Kitty," said Horace. He tried to catch Bud. Bud darted away. Horace trundled after him. Bud ran home to Gribble's front yard, stopped, and waited.

"Bud's playing tag with Horace," said Tilly.

Mr. Morris, from down the street, came by with his poodle, Beauty. "Hi, Jeff," he said. "I didn't know you had a baby brother." Mr. Morris was elderly and rather short-sighted.

"I don't," said Jeff. "We're babysitting Horace."

"Oh, my!" said Mr. Morris. "Aren't you brave?"

Beauty saw Bud. She growled and yapped

and leaped around on the end of her leash.

"That cat's always teasing Beauty," grumbled Mr. Morris. "He knows she's on a leash and can't catch him."

Bud scooted under the bushes next to Gribble's house. Beauty thought she'd won and settled down. Horace bent double like a sandwich board to look for Bud.

"What a cute dog," said Tilly Perkins. She petted Beauty.

"Is Jeff babysitting you, too?" asked Mr. Morris.

Tilly told Mr. Morris about her parents' trip to Africa.

Mrs. Fesku came home. "What are you all doing in the cat woman's yard?" she asked.

"Horace is trying to catch Bud," Tilly said.

Bud peered out from under the bushes to tease Horace.

"Kitty," said Horace. "Want kitty."

"Don't touch it," cried Mrs. Fesku. "It might have fleas."

Beauty saw Bud. She began to yap and dance about.

"It isn't fair," grumbled Mr. Morris. "Beauty has to be on a leash. Why shouldn't cats be treated the same way? And licensed, like dogs. I'm going to write to the paper about it."

"Now you're talking," agreed Mrs. Fesku. "Write to the mayor as well. I'll speak to Mr. Brown. He's the mayor's assistant. And he can't hide away in City Hall like the mayor. He's right here where we can get at him."

"Poor Dad," said Jeff to Tilly later. "No wonder he's against cats. He'll never let me have one of Gladys's kittens."

Did Tilly Perkins give up hope?

Did Tilly Perkins give up trying?

No, she didn't. Tilly Perkins gave it another shot. "Keep your four-leaf clover safe, Jeff," she said. "Put it inside a book so it doesn't get squashed. Four-leaf clovers never fail."

Chapter 5

A Perfect Pet

The Browns and Tilly were eating breakfast in the Browns' big, sunny kitchen.

Tilly Perkins beamed at Mr. and Mrs. Brown. "Guess what?" she said. "Gladys is going to have kittens."

Jeff kicked her foot under the table. This was not a good time to ask about a kitten.

Tilly didn't feel his kick. Or, if she did, she didn't care. "Gribble says Jeff can have a kitten," she said. "She knows he'll give it a good home."

Mrs. Brown looked up from her cereal. "I'm

sorry, Tilly," she said. "But Jeff knows he can't have a cat." She glanced at Mr. Brown.

Mr. Brown looked up from his newspaper and scowled. "Cats, cats, cats. That's all I ever hear about," he said. He picked up his knife and slapped marmalade onto his toast. "Some people want to treat cats like dogs. Others say that would be cruelty to animals. I'm caught in the middle. There's no way we can have a cat in this family."

"Jeff's an only child," Tilly said. "Only children need pets for company. That's why I have so many. People will understand."

"No way," said Mr. Brown. "The cat haters will say I'm a cat lover. They'll say I can't be fair to both sides. They'll tell me to quit my job." He choked on a piece of toast. His face turned brick red.

Mrs. Brown thumped him on the back. "Don't upset yourself, dear," she said. "It's not good for you."

"You needn't thump so hard, Gabby," said Mr. Brown. "I'm okay now. Jeff, how about a goldfish instead?"

"Goldfish are pretty," said Tilly Perkins. Her eyes looked dreamy. "Like drops of sun floating in the water. But you can't cuddle one."

"A hamster," said Mrs. Brown.

"Hamsters aren't playful, like kittens," said Jeff.

"A budgie bird," said Mr. Brown. "They talk, if you're lucky."

"I think it's cruel to keep birds in cages," said Mrs. Brown.

"A puppy would be okay," said Jeff.

"We can't have a dog," said Mr. Brown. "We've talked about it before. We're gone all day, to work and to school. A dog would get too lonesome."

"If you want a perfect pet, get a cat," said Tilly Perkins. "That's my advice."

"Come to think of it," Mr. Brown said thoughtfully, "a cat might get rid of some of those mice in Jeff's room. That's a plus." He meant the tame white mice that Tilly had given Jeff for his birthday.

Tilly Perkins's eyes twinkled. "Mr. Brown, you're teasing," she said.

"Anyway, the mice are safe in their glass cage," said Jeff. "I wouldn't let my cat into Mouse Town."

"Well, we'll see," said Mr. Brown. "Wait until the cat question dies down at City Hall. Then we'll talk about it again."

Tilly Perkins winked at Jeff.

"We're not making any promises," said Mrs. Brown. "Don't get your hopes up, Jeff."

"All the same," said Tilly Perkins, when she and Jeff were alone, "it's a good sign."

Chapter 6

Around the Bend

On Sunday afternoon, the Browns decided to have a barbecue.

"It's a warm day for May," said Mrs. Brown. "Just right for a barbecue."

Mr. Brown tied on his apron. "This is the life," he said, as he stuffed the salmon. "No mayor calling for this, that, and the other thing. No angry letters about cats. No furious phone calls about cats. Just good food and good company. Sunday is my favorite day of the week." He hugged Mrs. Brown and grinned at Jeff and Tilly.

Mrs. Brown made the salad. Jeff and Tilly set the picnic table and made a pitcher of lemonade. Then everybody sat down to have a cool drink while the salmon finished cooking. A loud screech made them jump out of their chairs.

"What in the world was that?" asked Mrs. Brown.

The Browns had a tall fence around their backyard to make it private. Someone shook the garden gate. It rattled as if it might come off its hinges. Mr. Brown strode across the lawn to open it.

"Mrs. Fesku," he said, "what's wrong?"

"I'll tell you what's wrong," cried Mrs. Fesku. She shook something green under Mr. Brown's nose.

Mr. Brown wrinkled his nose and took two steps backwards.

Mrs. Fesku followed Mr. Brown. "It's those cats," she yelled. "They dug up two of my geranium plants. I planted four dozen. It took me all day."

Every spring, Mrs. Fesku planted flowers.

Red, white, red, white, red, white down both sides of the front path. Always the same. *Boring,* thought Jeff.

"They were coming along nicely," said Mrs. Fesku, "until those cats did their dirty work." She looked as if she might burst into tears.

"Come and sit down, Mabel," said Mrs. Brown. She put her arm around Mrs. Fesku's shoulders and led her to a chair. "Have a cool drink." She poured a glass of lemonade for Mrs. Fesku.

"Don't try to butter me up," said Mrs. Fesku, with a sob. "I want something done."

"Like what?" asked Mr. Brown.

"Like making that woman get rid of those cats," said Mrs. Fesku. "Filthy things."

In a friendly way, Tilly Perkins perched on the arm of Mrs. Fesku's chair. "Cats are actually very clean," she said. "When they go to the bathroom, they're very careful to cover it up. I expect that's how they dug up your plants, Mrs. Fesku. They didn't mean to. It's only natural for them."

"I don't need a lecture on the habits of cats, thank you, Tilly Perkins," said Mrs. Fesku.

Did Tilly Perkins go away in a huff?

Did Tilly Perkins go away in a sulk?

No, she did not. Tilly stayed right where she was and spoke sweetly. "Your flowers are very beautiful, Mrs. Fesku," she said. "Couldn't you put in a few more?"

"We'll help," added Jeff. He wanted to stop Mrs. Fesku from being angry. Then maybe she'd forgive Gladys and the other cats. He knew what "get rid of" meant.

Mrs. Fesku looked sulky. "Do you know how much geranium plants cost?" she asked.

I wouldn't give two cents for them, thought Jeff. But he decided it was wiser not to say so.

"Maybe Mrs. Gribble will pay for them," said Mrs. Brown.

Tilly Perkins shook her head. "I don't think she can afford it," she said. "Gribble has a lot of cats to feed."

Mrs. Fesku gave a sort of screech. "That's just what I'm complaining about. Those cats!

You're the mayor's assistant," she said to Mr. Brown. "Why don't you *do* something?"

"It's not as easy as you think," said Mr. Brown. "People have different ideas on the subject."

"Not the people around here," said Mrs. Fesku. "We all agree. That woman has too many cats."

Tilly Perkins gave a great, gusty sigh. "Poor Gribble doesn't have any kids. That's why she loves her cats so much."

"If she's so fond of her cats, she should keep them home," Mrs. Fesku snapped. She leaped out of her chair and shook her wilted flowers at Mr. Brown. "You can tell the mayor that we want action. Cat action! And we want it soon." She swept out of the yard, banging the gate behind her.

Mr. Brown looked grim. He went to inspect the barbecue. "I suppose our salmon is totally ruined," he said. "Like my Sunday."

"Meow," said a cat voice. It came from the top of the fence. Gladys gazed down at the Browns' barbecue.

"Gladys wants to come to the barbecue," Jeff said. As he spoke, Luther tiptoed along the fence. A second later, Bud came up to join him. The twins followed. They sat in a row and licked their lips.

"They don't mind eating ruined salmon,"said Tilly.

"Grrrr," growled Mr. Brown. "Cats!" He rushed at the fence waving his barbecue fork. "I'll give them salmon if I get hold of them," he barked.

The cats fled. Gladys yelled some rude remarks in cat language as she went.

Mrs. Brown looked worried. "Your father's behaving like a mad dog, Jeff. It's this cat business. It's driving him crazy. Not another word to him about cats, either of you. And that's an order."

Chapter 7

SALLY'S
LEGAL ADVICE
SERVICE
555-7132

Cat on the Roof

"Here kitty, kitty, kitty. Here kitty, kitty, kitty," called Gribble. She was standing in the Feskus' front yard.

Jeff and Tilly were on their way home from school. Poppy Rose, Bruno, and Sally were with them. They were going to play on Jeff's trampoline for awhile.

"What's the cat woman doing?" asked Bruno.

Jeff chuckled. "Luther must be on the Feskus' roof again," he said. "Sometimes he climbs up the trellis on the side of their house."

"Spidercat!" said Bruno.

When they got closer, Tilly looked up. "That's not Luther," she said. "That's Gladys."

Gladys walked along the top of the roof and looked down at Gribble. She mewed pitifully, like a kitten. Only she wasn't a kitten.

"She's going to be a mother," Tilly said.

"What's wrong, Gribble?" asked Jeff. "Why won't she come down?"

"She's scared," said Gribble. "Wouldn't you be?"

"Why did she go up in the first place?" asked Bruno.

"She followed Luther," said Gribble. "Mr. Morris's poodle chased them. He let her off the leash."

"Why didn't she follow Luther back down again?" asked Bruno.

"When he wants to come down, Luther runs down the high roof," Jeff said. "Then he jumps down from that little roof over the front door. But Gladys isn't as young and athletic as Luther."

"Fat cat," said Sally.

"Silly cat, too," said Bruno. "Come on, Jeff. I want to try out that trampoline."

"We can't leave Gladys up there," said Tilly Perkins. "The roof is hot today. She'll be thirsty."

"She might die," said Poppy Rose.

"That'll teach her not to climb up houses,"said Sally.

"If the Feskus come home, they'll be mad,"said Jeff.

"They might sue you," Sally said to Gribble. "I'll be glad to represent you in court. Here's my business card."

"Stop blathering," said Gribble. "A person can't think."

"Get a ladder," said Poppy Rose. "Jeff can climb up and bring Gladys down."

Jeff looked up the side of the house to the roof peak. "It's pretty high up there," he said.

"Chicken," said Bruno. He made clucking noises and flapped his elbows.

"Jeff might fall off," said Sally. "Then his parents could sue the Feskus. Or should it be Gribble? I'll have to check with my dad. In any case, Jeff, here's my card."

"Nobody's climbing up any ladders,"

croaked Gribble. "There must be another way. If only I could think of it."

"Send for the fire department," said Poppy Rose.

"They won't come," said Gribble. "They get too many cat calls. They say they might be away when a fire alarm comes in."

"Wait until your dad gets home, Jeff," said Poppy Rose. "He can climb up and get the scaredy cat."

That's not a good idea, thought Jeff. *Mom said cats were driving Dad crazy. If I ask him to rescue Gladys he might go into orbit. Then I'll have no hope of ever having a kitten.* "Mrs. Fesku will be home before my dad," he said.

"We could throw rocks," said Bruno. "That'll make her jump." He bent down to find one.

"Stop!" cried Tilly Perkins. "You'll scare her and she'll fall off the roof."

"Cats have nine lives," said Bruno. "She'll land on her feet."

"No, she won't," said Tilly. "Not from that height."

"Don't worry," said Sally. "Bruno couldn't

hit a barn door. He'd miss and break one of the Feskus's windows. Then . . ."

"We know," Jeff interrupted. "The Feskus would sue Bruno's parents."

"Okay," said Bruno. "Get a rope. I'll make a lasso and rope that cat."

"You'll miss her and rope the chimney," said Sally.

"Forget it, Bruno," Jeff said. "We don't want to make the Feskus even madder."

Did Tilly Perkins leave Gladys to her fate?

Did Tilly Perkins leave someone else to solve the problem?

No, she did not. Tilly Perkins never left a job undone. "Let's use Jeff's trampoline," she said. "Gladys can jump down onto it. That way she won't get hurt."

"Bet you a million dollars she won't jump,"said Bruno.

Gladys gazed down at them and howled for help.

Chapter 8

More Cats!

"**S**he looks too scared to jump," said Poppy Rose.

"Fraidy cat," said Sally.

Did Tilly Perkins throw in the towel?

Did Tilly Perkins throw up her hands?

No, she did not. Tilly Perkins threw herself into the task. "First we'll get the picnic table," she said. "We can stand on that and hold the trampoline up. Then we'll be closer to Gladys."

"Good idea," said Jeff. "Gribble, why don't you get one of Gladys's favorite cookies? We'll put it on the trampoline. That'll tempt her to jump."

Gribble rushed away to get them. She moved fast in her sneakers and Bermuda shorts.

"Is the trampoline heavy?" asked Poppy Rose.

"It's only a one-person trampoline," said Jeff. "Five of us can easily hold it up."

"Six," said Sally, "counting Gribble. It's her cat."

"Gribble doesn't have to help," said Jeff. "She's not young and nimble like Luther. She's more like Gladys."

The trampoline was still not high enough for Gladys to jump onto.

"Let's borrow the Feskus' picnic table," said Jeff. "Someone help me carry it."

Between them, Bruno, Jeff, Sally, and Poppy Rose carried the picnic table from the Feskus' backyard to the front.

"Phew!"panted Bruno. "That cat sure is a lot of trouble."

Gribble came back with a whole bag of

cookies. She brought a chair and used it as a step. One, two, three, and she was up on the picnic table. *I was wrong,* thought Jeff. *Gribble is like Luther.*

"One, two, three, heave," cried Tilly.

Up went the trampoline high over their heads. Gladys put her head on one side and looked down at it. "Meow, ow, ow," she wailed.

"Snack time, Gladys," called Gribble.

"Jump, Gladys!" cried Tilly. "We'll catch you."

"Hurry up," cried Sally. "My arms are getting tired."

"Yucky," said Poppy Rose. "She's drooling all over the trampoline."

"Jump!" yelled Bruno.

Gladys jumped.

"Bull's eye," said Bruno.

Before they could lower the trampoline, Gladys leaped down to the table. She didn't even stop for the cookie. From the table, she jumped to the ground. Gribble had left the bag of cookies lying there. Gladys pounced on the bag. She tried to stick her head inside it. The bag slithered around. Gladys tossed it into the air. Cookies spilled out of the bag.

Luther, Bud, and the twins appeared from nowhere. They joined in the game. Luther used all four feet.

Gribble hopped down from the table. "Bad cats. Give me those," she cried. She snatched the bag away from them.

The cats thought it was part of the game. They chased the spilled cookies and batted them around.

"Way to go," yelled Bruno. "Soccer cats."

No one noticed Mrs. Fesku arrive home with Horace. "What's going on here?" she demanded.

Gribble didn't answer. "Scoot," she boomed. The cats ran for home. Gribble took off after them.

Jeff had to explain.

Mrs. Fesku did not look pleased. "I'm tired of those cats," she said, "howling and dancing on my roof. It's worse than a rock concert."

"Cool cats," said Sally.

"Gladys isn't to blame, Mrs. Fesku," Tilly said. "Mr. Morris's dog chased her."

Mrs. Fesku didn't answer. "Horace," she screamed. "Drop that cookie. You don't know where it's been."

"It's okay," said Bruno. "It's one of the cat woman's cat cookies."

Mrs. Fesku raced to Horace. She grabbed the cookie out of his hand. Horace started to yell.

"Dirty!" said Mrs. Fesku with a shudder. She scrubbed Horace's hand with a tissue.

Round tears ran down Horace's round cheeks.

"Don't worry, Mrs. Fesku," said Tilly Perkins. "It's not really a cat cookie. Gribble gives her cats people cookies."

"I don't care what she gives them," said Mrs. Fesku. "Horace isn't eating one."

Horace opened his mouth to a big, round "O" and wailed louder than ever.

"Gribble shouldn't feed cookies to her cats," said Poppy Rose. "That's why Gladys is too fat to jump."

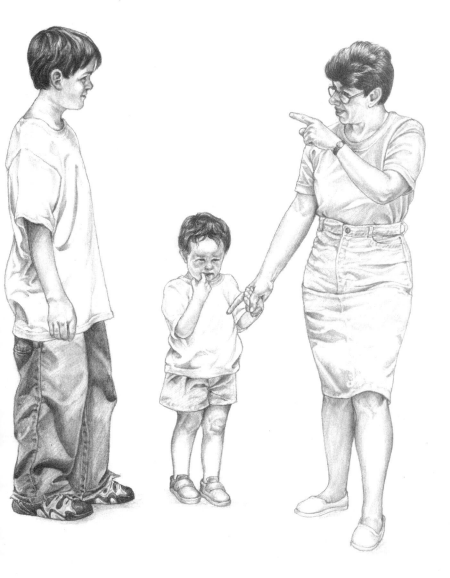

"She's not fat," said Tilly. "She's pregnant."

"I might have known." Mrs. Fesku wailed almost as loudly as Horace. "More cats! That's all I need." She shook her finger at Jeff. "Your dad's going to hear more about this. You can tell him that from me." She swept up the howling Horace and marched into the house.

"Mom and Dad will never let me have a kitten now," said Jeff. "Mrs. Fesku will make sure of that. She'll send Dad right out of his mind."

"I told you, Jeff," Bruno said. "You should've wished for a dirt bike."

"Forget it," said Sally. "Wishing on a four-leaf clover is a waste of time."

"It's the kind of idea that Tilly Perkins *would* come up with," said Poppy Rose.

"Wishes *do* come true," Tilly said. "Sometimes you just have to wait a bit."

Chapter 9

Fesku for Mayor

The next day they were in Jeff's backyard playing on the trampoline. Bruno jumped so high he could see the Feskus' front yard.

"It looks like the Feskus' front lawn has sprouted giant mushrooms," he shouted.

"Let me see," said Poppy Rose. "It's my turn." She did a few warm-ups, then a giant spring. "They look like 'For Sale' signs," she said.

"I bet they're 'Vote for Fesku' signs," said Sally. "Mr. Fesku's running for mayor. He told my dad. He said the mayor and council are a waste of time. They're always talking about a new cat law, but they never pass one. Mr. Fesku says he'll light a fire under those people at City Hall."

"He can forget it," said Jeff. "My dad wouldn't want to work for Mr. Fesku."

"He won't have to," said Sally. "Mr. Fesku says when he's mayor, he'll fire your dad."

Tilly Perkins put her hand on Jeff's shoulder. "Don't worry, Jeff," she said. "No one will vote for Mr. Fesku."

"Who says?" said Bruno. "We'd better check out those signs."

They trooped out of the yard and stopped outside the Feskus' place to read the signs.

ENOUGH TALK. ACT NOW.

TREAT CATS LIKE DOGS—LICENSES

ONE CAT PER HOUSE

RETRAIN CATS

VOTE FESKU FOR MAYOR—HE'LL GET THE

JOB DONE!

"Retrain cats?" said Poppy Rose. "What's he going to teach them?"

"Typing," said Sally. She giggled. "Can't you just see them, with their little paws."

"Dipstick!"said Bruno. "It means teach them not to go to the bathroom in other people's yards."

"Fesku will do the job," said Poppy Rose.

She and Sally staggered around, laughing.

Mrs. Fesku came out of the house. "What are you laughing at?" she asked.

Before they could answer, Gribble came out of her house. She stomped down the sidewalk and stopped to read the signs.

Gribble scowled. "Cat licenses!" she boomed in her bullfrog voice. "How's a person supposed to pay for those?" Her scowl got worse. "One cat per house! What a crazy idea! This is a free country, isn't it?"

She glowered at the signs again."Retrain cats! Phooey! Cats aren't circus animals." Then she stomped back home again.

Gribble's the only person I know who can stomp

in house slippers, thought Jeff, *especially fluffy blue ones with bobbles.*

Mrs. Fesku looked a bit red in the face. "I guess we left out a letter," she said. "It should say 'RESTRAIN,' not 'RETRAIN.' I'll get the marker."

Nobody waited to see her do it. The others went home. Tilly and Jeff threw a softball to one another and talked things over. Jeff felt sad and mad at the same time. "Grown-ups tell us not to fight. Why do they?"

Did Tilly Perkins look sad?

Did Tilly Perkins look sorry?

No, she did not. Tilly Perkins looked on the bright side. "Don't worry, Jeff," she said. "If your dad loses his job, he won't have to think about being fair," she said. "Then you can have a kitten. Four-leaf clovers always work."

"Oh, no!" Jeff groaned.

Chapter 10

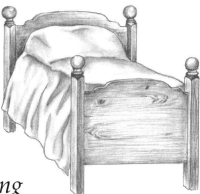

Gladys Is Missing

Tilly played hopscotch on the sidewalk. Jeff watched her. He didn't feel like playing. He was thinking about the war over the cats. Today, the mayor and council were having a meeting to discuss the cat problem. They would decide whether to require cat licenses and cat leashes.

Gribble's house looked shabby. Luckily, it was mostly hidden by trees and bushes. *Gribble can't afford paint*, thought Jeff. *How could she afford to buy cat licenses? How could she decide which cats to keep? She might have to find new homes for all of them.*

Gribble came up the street. She looked

worried. "Have you seen Gladys?" she asked. "I can't find her. She's close to having her babies, you know, so I've been keeping her inside. I don't want her to get hurt. But she slipped out of the door this morning. She's been gone all day."

Jeff's stomach did a somersault.

"Cats often hide somewhere to give birth," Tilly said. "They want to protect the newborn kittens."

"We'll help you look for her," said Jeff.

First, they checked Gribble's house from top to bottom. No Gladys!

"She might be in the forest," said Tilly. She meant the trees that grew on the hill across the street.

"You mean the trees," said Jeff.

"I've already looked there," said Gribble.

"We'll set up a search party," Jeff said. He phoned Bruno, Sally, and Poppy Rose.

"Where did that cat go now?" asked Bruno.

"If she has her kittens at the Feskus' place, there'll be trouble," said Sally. "As your lawyer, I'd better be there to advise you."

"I can give you a half-hour," said Poppy

Rose. "Then I have to try out for a TV commercial."

They all met in Jeff's bedroom to plan the search.

"Okay," said Bruno. "Let's beat the bushes."

"Gribble already has," said Jeff. "Anyway, we're not allowed to go in the trees alone."

"We won't be alone," said Bruno. "We'll be together."

"Not to put too fine a point on it,"said Sally. "That's begging the question."

"What's she talking about?"asked Bruno.

"If you're going in the trees, I have to beg off," said Poppy Rose. "My mother will have a fit if I mess up my hair."

"Listen," said Tilly Perkins. "I thought I heard a little meow."

This time they all heard it. It came from under Jeff's bed.

"Be very quiet," whispered Tilly Perkins. "Let Jeff look. It's his bed."

Gladys was curled up in an old sweater that Jeff thought he'd lost. Close to her were three tiny kittens. At least, he thought there were three. He couldn't see them very well because Gladys kept her body curled around them. The others took turns peeking under the bed.

"Don't touch the kittens," Tilly warned them. "Or she might kill them."

"Gross!" said Poppy Rose.

"It isn't gross," Tilly said. "It's only natural. It's the way cats are made."

Poppy Rose dusted herself off. "You should clean your room more often, Jeff," she said. "Then you wouldn't get kittens under the bed."

"They're so cute," said Sally. "As your lawyer, Jeff, I'd say you've got yourself a litter of kittens. Finders keepers, and all that legal stuff."

"I can't keep Gladys and her kittens," Jeff said. "Dad won't let me."

"You can bring her to my place if you'd like, Jeff," Bruno said. "There's lots of junk under my bed."

"We have to take her home," Jeff said.

"Gribble's worried about her. I wonder why Gladys didn't have her kittens at home."

Did Tilly Perkins look puzzled?

Did Tilly Perkins look bothered?

No, she did not. Tilly Perkins looked delighted. "Gladys trusts you, Jeff," she said. "She wants you to have one of her kittens. That's why she came to you."

Jeff felt a warm glow spread through his body, from inside to outside. Gladys trusted him. Knowing that felt almost as good as having one of her kittens. "Maybe my wish will come true, after all," he said.

Chapter 11

Some People Don't Deserve Cats

"What did the mayor and council members decide, dear?" asked Mrs. Brown at suppertime. "Did they pass a cat law?"

"Sort of," said Mr. Brown. "It isn't quite a law yet. The lawyers have to write it. There won't be any leashes. Cats on leashes would look silly. People in other towns and cities would laugh at us. But there will be a limit of two cats per household. Cats will have to wear tags. Any cat found without one will be taken to the pound."

"But that's awful!" cried Jeff. "The cats will be killed."

"Or adopted," said Mrs. Brown.

"People can't adopt all the cats without licenses," Jeff said. "There aren't enough homes for cats now. That's why Gribble has so many."

Did Tilly Perkins lose her temper?

Did Tilly Perkins lose her grip?

No, she did not. She seemed to be lost in thought.

"Jeff and Tilly, try to understand," said Mrs. Brown. "It's not that the Feskus are bad people."

"No," agreed Tilly. "Mrs. Fesku loves flowers and things that grow."

"And she loves Horace," Jeff said. "She just doesn't understand him very well. Poor Horace. He'll never be allowed to have a kitten either."

"If Gribble can't keep all her cats, I'll take some home. They can live on our farm," Tilly said.

"You'd better take all the kittens," said Jeff. "Gribble can't keep all of them. And Gladys will have to go with them. They're too young to leave their mother. That means I'll hardly ever see her anymore. Stupid cat law." Then he went to his room where he could have a good cry in private. After a while, he heard a tap on his door.

"Jeff, it's Tilly," she said. "Can I come in?"

"As long as you don't try to cheer me up," Jeff said. "There are some things you just have to feel sad about."

"I know," Tilly said. "I'm sorry about the cats."

Jeff blew his nose and let her in.

"People like the Feskus don't deserve to have cats around," Tilly said. "I'll ask Gribble to let me take all of them to the farm."

"What about Gribble? How will she feel?" Jeff asked.

"Let's go talk to Gribble," said Tilly Perkins.

Jeff and Tilly walked over to Gribble's house. They explained the cat situation to her.

Gribble looked glum. "Cat licenses!" she croaked. "Those people in City Hall think folks are made of money."

"Meow," said Gladys mournfully.

Her kittens climbed all over her. One was black with white spots. One was calico, just like Gladys. One was ginger. Jeff wouldn't let himself think about which kitten he would choose. It was too painful. But he knew anyway.

Luther didn't run up the curtains, or balance on a chair back. Bud didn't pretend to catch mice. The twins didn't try to catch each other's tails.

"Don't worry," Tilly said. "I'll take your cats and give them a good home on the farm."

At first Gribble scowled, then she nodded. "I might take a little holiday," she said. "My sister's been wanting me to visit. I could use a change from all the fuss and bother over a few cats."

Gribble *did* deserve a holiday, but Jeff was shocked. How could she give up her cats so easily?

The next day was Sunday. He woke up early. Had Mr. Fesku's motorcycle awakened him? No, it was the Perkins's pick-up truck. It came pop, pop, pop up the street like firecrackers exploding. Jeff heard Tilly run downstairs to greet her parents, who had just returned from Africa.

The Perkins family stayed for breakfast. Mr. and Mrs. Perkins wore their safari outfits. Mr. Perkins's safari hat was too big for him. It looked funny, but Jeff didn't feel like laughing. After breakfast, everybody but Jeff helped Gribble load the cats into cat carriers.

"We'll take you to visit the cats at Tilly's farm, Jeff," Mrs. Brown promised. She put her arm around his shoulders.

"They'll be happy there," said Mr. Brown. He cleared his throat.

Jeff pulled away from his mother's hug.

"The cats think they're going away to summer camp," croaked Gribble. "They're quite looking forward to it."

Bruno came out of his house. "I've come to see the last of those pesky cats," he said.

I'm the only one who cares, thought Jeff. *There's Mrs. Fesku at the screen door. And Horace.*

"Out," screamed Horace. "Kitty," he yelled. "See kitty."

Horace will miss the cats, thought Jeff. *Horace is a good kid.* Then he went upstairs to throw

away his four-leaf clover. It looked pretty brown and wilted. What good was it now? When had it ever been any good? He stared at it for a long time. Somehow, he couldn't quite bring himself to throw it away. He put it back in his drawer.

Chapter 12

Mice in Trouble

About a week later, Tilly Perkins showed up at school with several boxes. "Jeff, I brought you some mice," she said.

Jeff was in the schoolyard with Bruno.

"Jeff doesn't need mice," said Bruno. "He already has a zillion mice. You always give people pet mice for their birthdays, Tilly Perkins."

Did Tilly Perkins get the message?

Did Tilly Perkins get it through her head?

No, she did not. Tilly Perkins got a twinkle in her eye. "These aren't pet mice," she said. "They're barn mice. They have babies, so I brought their nests with them. You can have some, too, Bruno."

"Bruno and I don't have barns," Jeff said. "Why don't you keep them?"

"Because Gribble's cats are living in our barn," said Tilly. "Cats and mice don't mix."

"I thought you said it was natural for cats to catch mice," Jeff said.

"Of course," agreed Tilly. "But the poor babies don't stand a chance. They need a safe start in life. And you don't have any cats around to bother them."

Tilly Perkins likes mice, thought Jeff. *She likes them almost as much as she likes cats.*

"You don't need a barn," Tilly said. "A garage will do, or a garden shed."

"The Feskus have a garage," said Bruno. "And a shed. And a garden with lots of vegetables. Their place is perfect for mice. I'll help you with them after school, Jeff."

"Thanks, Bruno," Tilly said. "I can't help Jeff because I have to go home on the school bus."

Sally and Poppy Rose arrived at school.

"What's in those boxes?" asked Poppy Rose.

"Mice," said Bruno.

"Are they cute?" asked Poppy Rose. She peered over Jeff's shoulder.

"These aren't pet mice," said Jeff. "They're barn mice."

"You brought *barn* mice on the school bus?"asked Sally. "They might have escaped. They might've run over people's feet. And up their legs. Everybody would have screamed. The bus driver would've had a fit. You could've caused an accident. What you need, Tilly Perkins, is a good lawyer. I'll give you my card."

"Don't you dare let those mice escape in school, Tilly Perkins," said Poppy Rose, "or I'm telling."

"I won't let them escape," said Tilly. "They'd be scared."

"We're taking them to the Feskus' place after school," said Bruno. "You two can help."

"They'll be safe at the Feskus," said Jeff.

"Until the Feskus find out," said Poppy Rose.

"The mice will be grown up by then,"said Tilly. "They can run away."

"Let me think about the legal side of all this," said Sally. She gazed at the sky for a moment. Then she nodded. "Brilliant, Tilly Perkins," she said. "I couldn't have come up with a better idea myself."

I didn't know that Sally and the others cared so much about mice, thought Jeff.

After school, Poppy Rose, Sally, and Bruno helped him carry Tilly's mice home.

"One good thing about wild mice," said Jeff, "is that you don't have to worry about them. They can feed and water themselves. And you don't have to clean out their houses. Not like pet mice."

So Jeff and the others popped the mice under the Feskus' garden shed. They would find their own way inside. Then the kids went home and forgot about the mice.

A few weeks later, Mrs. Fesku was in her garden picking vegetables. Horace was helping. He kept picking the wrong ones.

"No, Horace," said Mrs. Fesku.

"Wah!" yelled Horace.

Jeff got tired of hearing them. He stood on a

LETTUCE

box and looked over the fence. "Hi, Horace. Want me to give you a push on my old swing?" he asked.

Horace grinned. "Nice kitty," he said.

I wish, thought Jeff. *I still miss having Gladys around to talk to. I miss watching Bud pounce on imaginary mice. I miss Luther and his Spiderman act. I even miss the twins chasing one another.* "Sorry, Horace," Jeff said. "No kitty." He lifted Horace over the fence.

"Thank you, Jeff," said Mrs. Fesku. "Horace doesn't understand gardening." She stood up. "I don't understand, either. We have a very poor garden this year."

That's true, thought Jeff. Usually the Feskus' vegetables grow in neat rows, shoulder to shoulder, like soldiers. This year, there are gaps. Maybe the vegetables had a battle.

"We must have garden pests," complained Mrs. Fesku. She picked a tomato. "This looks as if a mouse has been at it."

That was when Jeff remembered the mice. *They're getting lots to eat,* he thought. *Tilly will be pleased.* Mrs. Fesku went on picking vegetables. Jeff went on swinging Horace.

Mr. Morris came up the back lane. He called over the gate to Mrs. Fesku. "How is your garden this year?"

"Terrible," said Mrs. Fesku. "It's all chewed up."

"Same here," said Mr. Morris. "But we have a bumper crop of mice."

Oh, no! thought Jeff. *Poppy Rose was right. Now the mice will be in trouble.*

Mrs. Fesku went to the gate to talk to Mr. Morris.

"Up," Horace ordered. "Up, up, up."

The swing creaked and squeaked. Jeff couldn't hear what Mrs. Fesku and Mr. Morris were saying.

Chapter 13

I've Lost Horace

"Don't worry, Jeff," said Tilly Perkins when Jeff told her about the mice. "I'll think of something. Maybe I should come over to your place this weekend."

When she arrived, Mrs. Fesku was just going out. "Tilly Perkins, come here a minute," she called.

"What's wrong, Mrs. Fesku?" Tilly asked. "Would you like us to babysit Horace?"

"No, thank you," Mrs. Fesku said. "I found a teenager this time. Horace is getting to be a bit of a handful. I think he needs someone older and firmer. I hope you don't mind."

"Not at all," said Jeff.

"Tilly, what happened to Mrs. Gribble's cats?" asked Mrs. Fesku.

"I took them to our farm," said Tilly.

"All of them?" asked Mrs. Fesku.

"Every last one," said Jeff. He blamed Mrs. Fesku for that.

"Horace misses them," said Mrs. Fesku.

"So do I," said Jeff. "And so does Gribble. When she got back from her vacation, she had mice in her house."

"I could bring Horace a kitten," said Tilly Perkins.

"No, thank you," said Mrs. Fesku.

Jeff and Tilly went to look for the mice. They couldn't find any. "Mice are good at hiding," said Tilly.

When they came back, a teenage girl stood on the Browns' doorstep. "I've lost Horace," she said, and burst into tears. "I was only on the phone for five minutes, honest," she said, between sobs. "I left him playing in the backyard."

"Don't cry," said Mrs. Brown. "He can't be far away. We'll help you find him. Jeff and Tilly, you look up and down the street. I'll take the back lane." She told the babysitter to ask at every house.

It didn't take long. Because of the tree-covered hill, Jeff's street had houses on only one side. There was no sign of Horace.

"I'll phone the police," said Mrs. Brown. She took the babysitter with her.

Tilly looked at the hill across the street. "Horace might be lost in the forest," she said.

"No way," said Jeff. "Even Horace couldn't climb that wall."

"It's high across the road," Tilly agreed. "But near the top of the street, it gets lower. Then it curves around at the top of the street and down this side. Remember, it runs along one side of Gribble's yard. It's a lot lower there."

Jeff nodded. "Right. Gribble's little wall wouldn't stop Horace. But I hope you're wrong. There's a busy road at the top of the hill. That's if Horace didn't fall in the trees and hurt himself."

"Let's go, Jeff," said Tilly. "We'll find him."

"Have you found Horace yet?" Mr. Morris called to them.

Mr. Morris and some of the other neighbors had come out of their houses. They all wanted to help find Horace.

"No," said Jeff. "We're going to look in the trees."

"Oh, no, you're not," said Mrs. Brown. She had finished talking to the police. "You two, stay put. We adults will do it."

"I'll bring Beauty," said Mr. Morris. "She's a regular bloodhound."

Gribble came out of her house. She didn't join the search party. The other adults didn't ask her to. Maybe they thought she wasn't nimble enough. Next, Bruno, Sally, and Poppy Rose turned up.

"Is it true?" asked Poppy Rose. "Is Horace lost?"

Jeff nodded.

"Maybe he's been kidnapped," said Sally.

Bruno looked scornful. "Who'd want to

kidnap Horace?" he said. "You couldn't give that kid away."

"He *looks* cute," said Poppy Rose.

The babysitter gave a howl of misery.

"Don't worry," said Sally. "As soon as the kidnappers find out what he's really like, they'll bring him back. The Feskus won't even have to pay a ransom."

Jeff saw a car coming. "Speaking of the Feskus," he said, "here they come."

The babysitter turned white. "I think I'm going to throw up," she said.

"Don't do it on Jeff's lawn," said Bruno. "He has to cut it."

"Gross," said Poppy Rose.

Mrs. Fesku got out of the car. She frowned at the babysitter. "Where's Horace?" she asked.

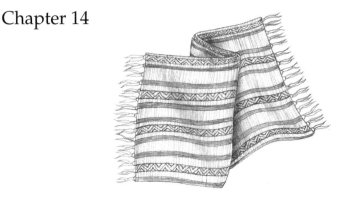

Chapter 14

Horace Jumps

The babysitter didn't answer. She sat on the grass and rocked back and forth, holding her stomach.

Did Tilly Perkins waste words?

Did Tilly Perkins waste her breath?

No, she did not. Tilly Perkins wasted no time. "Horace is lost," she said.

"Horace!" Mrs. Fesku screamed. "Oh, my poor baby. Where is he? What have you done with him?" She knelt down beside the babysitter and shook her.

"Stop that. You'll hurt her," croaked Gribble.

"The neighbors have made up a search party. They'll find Horace."

"A lot you care," said Mrs. Fesku, sobbing.

"Of course I care," snapped Gribble. "I know how I felt when Gladys was missing." She shivered and pulled her brightly colored Mexican shawl around her shoulders. "I still miss my beautiful cats."

"Horace isn't a cat," sobbed Mrs. Fesku. "He's a child."

Mr. Fesku got out of the car. "Mabel, what's taking the babysitter so long?" he called. "I'm waiting to take her home."

"She lost Horace," screamed Mrs. Fesku.

Mr. Fesku's mouth fell open. In the moment of silence that followed, they heard a voice.

"Here me am, Mommy," it said. "Here me am, Daddy." There was Horace on the top of the wall—the highest part. He spread out his arms. "Jump," he said. "See me, jump."

"No!" everyone shouted together. They all rushed across the road and stood under the wall.

"Stay there!" cried Mr. Fesku. "Daddy doesn't want to see you jump."

"Tell the search party," cried Tilly Perkins. "Help! We've found Horace," she called. "He's on the wall."

"Tilly Perkins will make them hear," said Jeff. "She's the best hog caller in the country."

"Wait, Horace," begged Mrs. Fesku. "Listen to Mommy. Daddy will come and get you. Stay there."

"I'll get the ladder," said Mr. Fesku.

"No," said Horace. "Me jump." He bent his knees.

"Gribble! Your shawl," yelled Jeff.

Gribble tore off her shawl. The other kids knew what Jeff had in mind. Not even Sally stopped to argue. They grabbed the shawl around the edges.

"We need cookies," yelled Poppy Rose.

"No, we don't," said Bruno. "Horace *wants* to jump—not like Gladys."

Mrs. Fesku looked horrified. "Horace can't jump into that," she cried.

"Gladys jumped onto the trampoline," said Jeff. "She made it."

"If Horace gets hurt, don't blame me," said Sally. "This is Jeff's idea. Sue his parents."

"Stop it, Sally," Jeff said. "Mrs. Fesku is worried enough."

"Here come the searchers," cried Tilly Perkins. "They'll save him. Horace, wait."

Three of the volunteers came through the woods. One balanced his way along the top of the wall.

But Horace was done waiting. "Two, one, *three*," he cried. And Horace jumped.

Chapter 15

Wishes Do Come True

"If Jeff hadn't thought of the shawl, Horace would have been killed," Tilly said. She had stayed to have a barbecue with the Browns, and she was telling Mr. Brown about Horace's adventure.

"Not really," muttered Jeff, blushing. "There were all those people standing around. Someone would have caught him."

"Maybe not killed," said Mrs. Brown. "But hurt. The wall is very high right there."

"It was quick thinking, Jeff," said Mr. Brown. "I'm proud of you."

"Does that mean I get a kitten?" Jeff asked.

Mr. Brown sighed and shook his head. "Sorry, son. The Feskus don't like cats and I don't want to upset our neighbors."

As he got up to light the barbecue, someone rattled the garden gate.

"Hello-o," called Mrs. Fesku. "It's me."

"Oh, no," groaned Mr. Brown. "What now? Let her in, Jeff."

"How's your garden?" asked Mrs. Fesku.

"We don't grow one," snapped Mr. Brown.

Mrs. Fesku looked around. "Pity," she said. "Ours is a mess. Mice, you know."

"So I suppose you want us to pass a mouse law at City Hall," growled Mr. Brown.

Dad's feeling grouchy, thought Jeff. *He hates to be interrupted when he's cooking.*

Mrs. Brown tried to make up for her husband's bad manners. "That's too bad," she said. "Mice can do a lot of damage. I hope they don't attack our fruit trees this winter. They eat the bark. If they eat too much, the trees die."

"We have fruit trees, too," said Mrs. Fesku. She frowned, thinking.

Mr. Brown waved his barbecue fork in the air. *Dad looks like Neptune, Roman god of the sea,* thought Jeff. *Or maybe Neptune's son, Triton. Either way, he looks dangerous.*

"Do put down that fork, dear," said Mrs. Brown. "You might hurt someone."

Mrs. Fesku backed away. "I don't think I ever thanked Jeff for rescuing Horace," she said. "How about a kitten as a reward? Tilly Perkins must have one to spare. You'd get it fixed, of course. We don't want too many cats in the neighborhood."

"True," said Mr. Brown.

"Gribble has mice in her house," said Tilly Perkins. "She needs a cat or two. Mice multiply fast. Soon they'll be looking for other houses to live in. It's only natural."

Mrs. Fesku shuddered. "Mice are a worse problem than cats," she said. She glared at Mr. Brown. "I want you to forget the cat law. And be quick about it, before those mice eat us out

of house and home. You're as slow as molasses in January down there at City Hall. By the way," she added, "my husband has decided not to run for mayor. He's too busy."

Mr. Brown stabbed a steak with his barbecue fork.

"Please, dear," said Mrs. Brown, "that's no way to treat a steak."

Mrs. Fesku hightailed it to the gate. "Tilly Perkins," she called, "don't forget to bring back a few cats. You shouldn't have taken them all away in the first place. Trust you to overdo things. We'll have the one Horace likes—Bud, I think it's called. It's kind of cute." She hurried to the gate and let herself out.

"Yea!" Jeff yelled in a whisper. "I get my kitten."

Tilly Perkins grinned. "What did I tell you, Jeff? Wishes *do* come true," she said. "Oh, I think I forgot to tell you. Poppy Rose and Sally each want one of the twin cats."

Jeff couldn't believe his ears. "And Bruno's folks say he can have Luther," he said.

"So, after supper, you'd better phone Sally

and Poppy Rose and Bruno," said Tilly. "They can help us set some live traps. We have to take those barn mice back to the farm. They have more places to hide there. If they stay here, the cats will eat them all."

Jeff groaned. "Tilly Perkins," he said, "you sure know how to keep people busy."